TRAVELER

ANDREA MONTICUE

Copyright © 2024 by Andrea Monticue

All rights reserved.

No part of this book may be reproduced or transmitted in any form or by any means, electronic or mechanical, except for the purpose of review and/or reference, without explicit permission in writing from the publisher.

Cover design copyright © 2024 by by Niki Lenhart
nikilen designs.com

Published by Water Dragon Publishing
waterdragonpublishing.com

ISBN 978-1-964952-31-4 (Trade Paperback)

FIRST EDITION

10 9 8 7 6 5 4 3 2 1

ACKNOWLEDGMENTS

I would like to thank the entire gang at the Monmouth Writers Group in Oregon:

Barbara Freeman, Carrie DeAtley, Eva Ditler, Lyndell Robinson, Keith Tierney, Eric Fisher, Andy Marks, Robert Lee, Josh Coleman, Jackie McCormick, Margaret Anderson, and Gail Oberst. Plus a few others who come in on an irregular basis.

Your critiques made me a better writer.

AUTHOR'S NOTE

Bob Schoonover was a very dear friend who was sadly taken from us far too early, and I still miss him. His widow requested that I add him as a character in one of my stories and I'm happy to be able to do that with this book.

Sail on, Bob.

TRAVELER

TUESDAY, JUNE 20TH
17:05 EDT
ETA: 2 DAYS, 1 HOUR, 19 MINUTES
NASA HEADQUARTERS, WASHINGTON, DC

"MA'AM, THE PRESIDENT IS CALLING," a young intern, standing half-in the door to the office, said in breathless anticipation. NASA Administrator Elizabeth Morrison wondered if the president or the news caused the breathlessness.

"Thank you, John. Send Dr. Schoonover in."

"Yes, Ma'am." Morrison sat down at her desk, straightened her spine, and clicked on the computer to start the conversation with the so-called Leader of the Free World.

The president's face appeared on the computer screen, and Morrison had to swallow the bile that wanted to climb up her esophagus and into her mouth. The man was not bad-looking, but he was a fascist pig who consorted with totalitarians. He had invoked the Insurrection Act, thrown out *habeas corpus,* and there were rumors of a Russian liaison.

"Liz, what is all this talk about aliens," The Man asked.

Morrison hated being called Liz, and she had to unclench her teeth before proceeding. "Sir, yesterday at 5:31 in the morning Eastern Daylight Time, there was an event about 7 billion miles from Earth, and one of our satellites picked up a short, low-intensity gamma-ray flash in the southern hemisphere."

"Liz, I don't want to know about X-rays from space. You told my chief of staff that you had a message about aliens."

"Gamma rays, sir. And I didn't say anything about aliens —"

"Get to the point, Liz. I'm kinda busy here with the ambassador from Syria."

"Sir, we've been watching that patch of sky for 23 hours now, and we've detected an object ..."

"What kind of object? Like a comet, or that cigar thing that went by a few years ago?"

"No, sir. But the thing is —"

"Liz, this better not be about my decision to replace you as administrator."

"No, sir. If you'll listen for a sec," Morrison had to spit it out quickly before the President could interrupt again. "The object is decelerating. At twenty-five times the force of gravity."

"Liz, look. So a comet is slowing down. I don't understand what you're talking about."

"If it were a natural object, it would be speeding up as it fell towards the sun. This object is slowing down. And it's slowing down at a rate that isn't natural. It has to be something that was built, and has engines."

"So, you *are* talking about aliens!" the President said.

Son of a ... "Sir, we don't know if there are aliens. We only know there is a spaceship. It's decelerating at 25 gravities. Tardigrades can survive that, but not anything the size of a human. It's probably an automated craft. But its origins are outside our solar system. It's currently more than three and a half billion miles away. That's farther away than Pluto. When we first detected it, it was traveling at nearly a quarter of the speed of light. We don't have that kind of technology. And it's headed straight for us!" Morrison nearly shouted that last part.

"And you say they're shooting ray guns at us?" Before Morrison could reply, the president muted his mic to talk to somebody else, leaving her to wonder why she bothered to vote.

The view in the computer screen shifted, and Morrison found herself looking at the Secretary of Homeland Security standing next to the President Even though he was an obsequious sycophant and white supremacist, he at least had an IQ higher than a department store's mannequin.

"Hello, Administrator Morrison. Dr. Randel Holzman here. Why did it take you a whole day to contact us about this?"

Dr. Schoonover had walked into Morrison's office and stood behind Morrison. "May I answer that question, Administrator?"

"By all means," Morrison gestured towards the computer screen. Instead of sitting down, Bob leaned over the computer station.

"Hi, Randel. Bob here," he said. "We did notify you. We followed all the protocols, but the event was 11 and a half billion kilometers away, so due to light-travel delay, we didn't know about it for 10 and a half hours. Also, we didn't know what we were looking at. That short gamma-ray flash Elizabeth told you about was followed by a constant radio noise at about 1000 gigahertz. It was a huge unknown, which we said in our initial briefing and every briefing after that. I'm sure it's in your inbox. We've been monitoring the radio source, and we've confirmed by its redshift that it's decelerating at 25 g's exactly."

Dr. Holzman whistled.

"And it's headed directly at us, Randel," Schoonover said with authority.

Dr. Holzman turned pale. "How fast will it be going when it hits us?"

"That's just it. It won't hit us. If the flight profile continues as it is, it will attain a zero velocity with respect to the Earth when it gets here."

"It's *landing*?" Holzman was incredulous.

"I don't believe it will land, but it'll probably go into Earth orbit."

Dr. Holzman pulled up a chair and sat in it, nearly knocking the President out of the way. "This is it, then. All those books and TV shows and movies about first contact, all those benevolent aliens and warmongering monsters, and we're living it now, for better or worse. Who else knows about this?"

"By now, the entire planet. As gamma-ray flashes go, it was loud, and other countries share our satellite data."

"Crap. When will it get here?"

"If the current trajectory doesn't change, it'll arrive at 6:24 PM on Thursday."

• • •

THURSDAY, JUNE 22
15:30 HOURS EDT.
TARGET DISTANCE FROM EARTH: 7.1 MILLION KILOMETERS
ETA: 2 HOURS 54 MINUTES

After spending the day in Washington D.C in one meeting after another, often with heated words, Dr. Robert Schoonover needed another shower and headed back to his hotel room followed by two young, serious MPs who parked themselves outside his room. While getting dressed, he clicked on the TV and a woman's voice could be heard giving the weather report. The banner on the bottom of the screen gave her name as Imani.

"As you can see through the weather cam, we still have thick haze from the Canadian wildfires, which will give us yet another spectacular sunset. The high-pressure zone sitting over western Kentucky and eastern Virginia is causing the winds to move in a clockwise manner, helping to bring in the wildfire smoke with that northwesterly flow. We are currently looking at poor air quality and a temperature of 88 degrees.

"For those of you hoping to get a look at the alien spacecraft that's arriving tonight, your best bet is to fly to the southern hemisphere, because that's where the scientists at NASA tell us it's headed. But if you're stuck here with the rest of us, keep in mind that the craft is still 4 million miles from Earth."

To emphasize this, a countdown of the miles was displayed in the lower right corner of the screen and updated every few seconds.

"We have telescopes and cameras sending images from Australia, South Africa, Argentina, and Antarctica, and we'll bring you the latest images. According to radar, the craft is nearly a kilometer long, which is huge for a spacecraft, but still tiny in terms of the distances involved, so no visual pictures are available. Back to you, Brad."

The excitement in the weatherwoman's voice was palpable. This was in contrast to the voices on the reality-challenged TV streams, where talking heads were screaming *hoax!* and blaming the other political party for using the red flag operation to tear down the fabric of society. The president had tried to keep the news a secret, but that quickly became pointless when Germany, then Australia, then Japan, and then half a dozen other nations broke the news.

Brad, the news anchor, took over the narration. "Not everybody is as excited about the aliens as Imani. There are reports of demonstrations all over the world. Some people claim to welcome the new alien overlords, while others herald the arrival of representatives of a benevolent galactic federation. Several scientists, including Radek Bostik, claim that the arrival of space aliens could only mean the downfall of civilization, that the aliens might start farming humans for food, or that they will turn humans into sex slaves, or that they were here to rescue their comrades at Area 51."

Dr. Schoonover cringed at not only the fringe science being reported, but also by the characterization of Radek Bostik a scientist. Calling Bostik a scientist was like calling a child with building blocks an engineer. He bought out promising start-up companies like *Celestech* and *EV Dynatech,* and had skill at hiring excellent engineers, but only his fans thought of him as any kind of scientist.

Brad the news anchor continued, "Earlier today, WOCD news host Andrew Vance interviewed a spokesman for the Save Our Earth Society. They assert that the aliens are from the Planet Nibiru and want to destroy the Earth in order to save their own planet from destruction in a collision. A huge contingent of people claimed that the aliens are already here in the form of reptilian shape shifters who control world governments and are responsible for wars, famine, and genocide."

None of these claims were as absurd as those which held that the aliens were messengers from God, here to announce the End Times, Schoonover thought.

Schoonover's attitude was to wait and watch. Attempting to contact the craft by radio on any frequency has proven fruitless, and scientists speculated wildly on the reasons. The most common was that it was an automated spacecraft, sent to gather data on Earth, and would leave just as silently, but the public found that idea boring. The only radio signal from the craft appeared to be noise without any modulation. Bob speculated that it was a by-product of the engine. It was more exhaust than signal.

Schoonover had his doubts. He had spent the latter part of his naval career in intelligence, and some oddities about this spacecraft raised his suspicious hackles. And he didn't believe for a minute that the craft would simply come to a halt half a kilometer above the ground, as some armchair mathematicians have suggested. It would have to change course eventually.

The television station switched back to more typical news and reported on how Jews, LGBT and those accused of being woke were losing their jobs as local governments concentrated on removing corruption from the public sector. The assumption was that if one were woke, then one was corrupt. *Habeas corpus* had been suspended in major cities, and lawsuits from states opposed to the president's agenda were summarily ignored. Armed paramilitary groups known collectively as Minute Men patrolled the streets of cities, arresting and often shooting anybody breaking curfew, engaging in petty crime, or simply for looking suspicious.

"The U.S. Supreme Court threw out a lawsuit, leaving intact an executive order forbidding states like California from restricting the sales of gasoline-powered vehicles. This is hailed by lobbyists as a huge win for the economy.

"Eco-terrorists, including Greenpeace and the Sierra Club, were arrested by the military while protesting in Washington, D.C. today.

"In international news, the dissolution of NATO continues as three more countries leave the organization. World leaders, such as Putin, Orbán, and Lukashenko, have joined the president in praising this as a major step towards lasting peace in Europe."

There was a knock on the door, and one of the MPs said, "Sir, your ride is here."

Schoonover clicked off the television, grabbed his briefcase, and opened the door. "Good. Let's not waste any more time."

The streets of D.C. were clogged with cars trying to get out of town, and they had been for three days. Survivalists had already gone to the wilderness and now many others were trying to join them. Emergency vehicles were also stuck in traffic, and Schoonover wondered how many people died simply because they couldn't get to the ER through this traffic. Schoonover shook his head in amazement. As if hiding out in the mountains was a good strategy against an enemy that could accelerate a kilometer-long spacecraft at 25 g's.

He was agog at the amount of energy that required.

Schoonover and his guards took the elevator to the roof where a helicopter awaited, and they flew five minutes to the White House lawn.

• • •

THURSDAY, JUNE 22
16:30 HOURS EDT.
TARGET DISTANCE FROM EARTH: 6.3 MILLION KILOMETERS
ETA: 1 HOUR 54 MINUTES
WHITE HOUSE

Schoonover was escorted into a large room filled with computer displays of maps and images from across the planet. One display showed the sky where the spacecraft would eventually appear. Another display showed the current distance and time to planetfall. Someone said, "If it doesn't change course, it'll land somewhere off the coast of Antarctica." Schoonover suppressed the urge to comment on how vague that was.

Randal Holzman waved to Schoonover as he entered, but he was otherwise ignored. There were a lot of politicians in the room, along with three generals and two admirals. One of the generals, William Phelps, was the Chief of Space Operations in the U.S. Space Force. He had a telephone handset in each hand and looked like he hadn't slept since Tuesday.

Schoonover caught snippets from various conversations:

"Carrier Strike Groups from the fifth and sixth fleets are underway, but they won't get there in time. Britain is sending a task group with the HMS *Prince of Wales.*"

"Argentina is sending the *ARA La Argentina* and she'll be in position within the hour."

"The International Space Station will be over Kamchatka when the spacecraft arrives."

Schoonover forced his way between people to get Holzman's attention. "Randel. I've got to talk to you."

"Hey, Bob. This'll have to wait. I've got Pac Fleet on the line."

"Randel, this is serious. The spacecraft isn't going to land in the Southern Sea."

Randel turned to him and looked suddenly attentive. "Has it changed course?"

"Not yet, but it will. I guarantee it."

"We can't take that chance."

"Think about it, Randel. A spacecraft that big can't land on the planet. It will establish an orbit and send landing craft. Probably robots."

"One minute, Bob. I've got to take this call."

Schoonover once again found himself ignored in a mob of busy people. He checked his phone for messages. There were hundreds of them, but none of them with the information he wanted to see. He didn't expect that the spacecraft would change course until its velocity was well under 100 kilometers per second.

"China is sending a carrier group. Russia is sending a single destroyer," a female voice said.

Schoonover understood the military response. Being paranoid was not at all unreasonable, but he doubted if any of the generals, admirals, or even cabinet members understood just how much energy the spacecraft could generate.

"One kilometer long," a man said. "That's enough room to carry thousands of soldiers and attack vehicles,"

"I doubt it," another said. "Most of that space is probably taken up by the engines and fuel reservoirs."

Finally! Schoonover thought. *Somebody who understands!* However, those engines did not resemble any earthly design. The exhaust wasn't hot. It was just radio noisy.

At T minus one hour, the distance display showed 1.6 million kilometers. Still four and a half times farther away than the moon.

"Bob, you wanted to talk to me?" Holzman said as he walked towards him.

"Yes. Yes, I do. Have your intelligence people figured out anything odd about this spacecraft?"

"Like what?"

"For instance, the deceleration is *exactly* 25 g's. To three decimal places."

"Why is that odd?" Holzman asked.

"Because That's an Earth-based constant. It's a measure of gravity on the Earth's surface. Why would an alien civilization that is capable of sending that spacecraft here use an Earth-based constant?"

Traveler

Holzman opened his mouth to say something and stopped, thought about it, and then said, "Good question."

Schoonover's phone buzzed and he looked at pulled it out to look at it.

"Is something wrong?" Holzman asked.

"Maybe. Nothing about this is normal. Text message from Elizabeth. Earlier today, when the spacecraft was still 200 million kilometers out, it launched some kind of ancillary craft."

"Wha... what kind of craft?"

"Like a boat or something," Schoonover said. "It's on a completely different trajectory."

"What's out there at that distance?"

"The asteroids."

Holzman thought about this and became angry. "Could the aliens send asteroids to crash on Earth?"

Schoonover was loath to stoke Holzman's paranoia, but he had to answer honestly. "Probably. But why would it?"

"To take over the Earth, of course!" Holzman was surprised that Schoonover even asked the question.

"If it wanted to take over the Earth, why would it destroy it?"

Holzman did that thing again, where he opened his mouth to say something then stopped. "Well, why else would they go to the asteroid belt?"

It, not they, Schoonover wanted to shout. He was still unconvinced that there were any aliens on that craft.

"Maybe it needs to mine the metals."

"They've changed course!" somebody shouted. Everybody's attention shifted immediately to the display of the spacecraft's trajectory. There wasn't much difference, but Schoonover could see by the accompanying numbers that it was significant. Somebody altered the scale on the display, and the new terminus of the trajectory became obvious: The Moon.

"You were right, Bob," Holzman said calmly and walked across the room to talk to an admiral.

• • •

FRIDAY, JUNE 23 00:00
TARGET DISTANCE FROM EARTH: LUNAR ORBIT
TIME SINCE TARGET ACHIEVED LUNAR ORBIT:
5 HOURS 35 MINUTES

The entire world watched their television sets and computer monitors as the traveler from the stars achieved lunar orbit, and the radio noise at 1000 gigahertz disappeared. Schoonover felt vindicated that he had guessed correctly about that. He also breathed a sigh of relief that the world's most powerful navies wouldn't be colliding in the Antarctic Ocean.

The spacecraft turned off its engines and became as silent as any space rock. However, amateur radio operators on Earth, and some large government operated ones, were sending messages of greetings or threats to it.

"What are they doing?" Holzman asked Schoonover.

"Orbiting the Moon."

"I mean, are they watching us? Listening to us? Evaluating us?"

"No idea," Schoonover said. "Probably all three. Maybe it's deciding what to do next."

Every telescope and most military radar units on the side of the Earth where the Moon was visible was aimed at it, but details were still sketchy. Lunar distances were too great, the velocity was too high, and the resolution of existing telescopes was too low.

"Are there any lunar satellites we can repurpose to image the craft?" somebody asked.

"Maybe the Lunar Reconnaissance Orbiter? It wouldn't be ideal, but we could rig something."

New conversations erupted concerning the technical difficulties and likely outcomes of such a task. Schoonover tried to contact both the Goddard Space Flight Center and the Ames Research Center, but they put him on hold.

"Why did it wait until the last minute to change course?" Randel asked.

"Maybe it didn't realize that the Earth was inhabited until then. But that seems unlikely. I'm sure they could detect all the radar we were beaming at it."

• • •

FRIDAY, JULY 28
01:30 HOURS EDT
TIME SINCE TARGET ACHIEVED LUNAR ORBIT:
35 DAYS, 7 HOURS, 5 MINUTES
MORRISON RESIDENCE

"It's been five weeks since the first confirmed extrasolar Traveler arrived in our solar system, and there has been, to date, no word from the aliens," the guy on BBC said. "No radio contact, no sign of aggression, nor a friendly gesture.

"NASA is continuing to weigh its options for a lunar launch, while China has announced a launch by next Friday. NASA Administrator Elizabeth Morrison insists that such a hasty launch would put astronauts at great risk."

Elizabeth closed her eyes and marveled that the news agency reported her words without elaboration or editorializing. That couldn't be said of Fauchs News, who insisted on turning her every word into a conspiracy. Not a day had gone by in the last five weeks when some news outlet hadn't called for an interview.

"Yet another person claimed earlier today to be the pilot of the spacecraft. We've lost count, but they range from being missionaries of peace to messengers of God insisting that we kill all the gays and heathens. This last one has been linked to several mass shootings in the U.S. and abroad."

Elizabeth had spent the past weeks surviving on junk food and very little sleep, and now sleep eluded her. She got up to take a Benedryl to facilitate drowsiness, but was distracted when her smartphone buzzed.

Another emergency? She wondered as she picked up the phone. There was a message from somebody who identified themselves as 1382. It contained a link to a file.

Worried that she would miss an important message, but leery that it was another attempt to scam her phone, she opened the message.

> 28 July 1600 GMT. This is important. Do not delete this text. Open the file.

Elizabeth read the message three times trying to make sense of it. *Who the hell was 1382?*

She deleted the message and then took the pills.

• • •

FRIDAY, JULY 28
10:58 HOURS EDT
TIME SINCE TARGET ACHIEVED LUNAR ORBIT:
35 DAYS, 16 HOURS, 33 MINUTES

"We don't have the resources or the money or the time or the technology to take a hundred people to the Moon," Morrison said to the computer screen. Commodore Patrick Atwater, an older British man listened to her glumly.

"My dear Administrator Morrison, I don't want you to do that. I simply want to impress upon you that the people who meet the spacecraft should represent more than the United States."

"Sir Atwater, do you know how many phone calls I've received with that same message from Mexico, Korea, India, Saudi Arabia, Italy, Sweden, and yes, even Russia? The entire planet wants to put diplomats on our mission."

"Yes, I see your point. It would be absurd. But certainly the special relationship between our two countries —"

There was a knock at the door and a young intern stuck her head in. "Administrator, we have a special communication from Goddard. They've picked up a message from the alien ... uh, spacecraft."

"Sir Atwater, I have to go."

"Agreed. I just received the same message. Shall we continue this conversation later?"

"Yes, later." She clicked the connection off and ran out the door. Bob Schoonover was standing in the center of a crowd of people, and they were all looking at a computer printout.

"What's going on, Bob?"

"Message from the craft. But nobody knows what it means."

"Can you explain?"

"What's to explain? It's simply a string of one thousand, three hundred eighty-two radio ticks."

Elizabeth's memory was tickled. That number sounded so familiar. Where had she seen it before? Then it hit her, and she needed to find a place to sit. "Bob, would you please send for someone who knows how to undelete a message on my phone?"

• • •

"You're very fortunate that the message wasn't overwritten," the young computer specialist said. "The linked file looks intact."

"What's in the file?" Bob asked.

"Not sure," the tech said. "It's huge. But the first words are, *Low-temperature mass rapid catalyst of CO_2 into C_2 products and oxygen.* Looks like a technical paper."

"Can you print it out? Also, send digital copies to the server," Elizabeth said.

"You got it."

"Bob, I was on the phone with Commodore Atwater, and he mentioned that they had also received the same message. What are the odds that Atwater also received a text in the dead of night?"

"Ask him?" Bob suggested.

"Not yet. Let's get this paper analyzed. In the meantime, I need to do something else." Morrison picked up her phone, found the undeleted message from 1382, and pressed *Call*.

Traveler

To her astonishment, the call connected and she heard it ring. A woman answered. "Do not ever call this number again. Erase the message and the file." There was a click, then silence.

• • •

**MONDAY, JULY 31
NOON, EDT
TIME SINCE TRAVELER ARRIVAL: 38 DAYS, 17 HOURS, 35 MINUTES**

The business offices of NASA in Washington, D.C. had an electrified feeling as engineers, astronauts, IT specialists, writers, and technicians all tried to work with subdued excitement. The biggest day in world history had come and gone and the anticipation for what the traveler would do next was expressed in nearly every conversation.

Conversations usually sounded something like: "Hey! Would you like to get some coffee and make warrantless speculations about what the traveler will do next?"

However, when the news broke about Radek Bostik, the world's richest billionaire, and owner of *StarDrive Technologies,* which supplied heavy-lift space rockets and crew modules for NASA, all the conversations changed.

"I'm announcing today, that in light of the news of the interstellar Traveler now silently orbiting the Moon, *StarDrive Technologies* will launch a moon rocket from our test base in the South Pacific in three days. I will personally rendezvous with the alien spacecraft and demand to know its intentions."

There were both standing ovations and comments about how jaw-droppingly stupid his plans were.

"He cannot be the spokesman for Earth," said one BBC news analyst. "He's a 42-year-old misogynistic, ultra-conservative billionaire man-child with more space toys than most nations. He's racing the Chinese to the Moon."

"Bostik, whose company, *Celestech,* effectively owns the Internet due to its dependence on the vast constellation of Celestech communications satellites, has stopped censorship of conservative voice in social media by buying the social networking service, Buzzstream," said an American analyst with obvious pride. "He is protecting American children by lobbying to criminalize homosexual and transgender behavior and healthcare, and now He's taking American capitalism to the Traveler."

• • •

TUESDAY, AUGUST 1
07:45 EDT
TIME SINCE TRAVELER ARRIVAL: 39 DAYS, 13 HOURS, 20 MINUTES

"Commodore, I'm not saying that we received a message, and I'm not saying that we didn't. Just suppose we did," Morrison said over the computer link to the U.K. This conversation had been going on for far longer than she expected it to. She was trying to be deferential to Sir Atwater by calling the U.K. in the early afternoon in England. "I would not like to think that we were the only ones who carried that burden."

"Then you should also suppose that we also received an SMS with a link to a file," Sir Atwater said. "And you should also suppose that it contained a link to a file on how to make fast rechargeable, high-capacity glass batteries."

Elizabeth quickly muted the mic and turned to her secretary. "Get the European Space Agency on the line. I want to talk to the Director General, and if they give you grief, you can tell them to kiss their ticket to the Moon goodbye. Then get Sakane Kazuja of JAXA in Japan on the line and tell them the same thing. Then we'll start with all the other space agencies on the planet."

The secretary and an intern passed each other at the door to Elizabeth's office just as she unmuted Sir Atwater. "Ma'am, China is launching a moon rocket."

"Yes, on Friday," she responded. Sir Atwater's gray, burly eyebrows raised a quarter inch.

"No! Now!"

"Did you know about this, Commodore?"

"Absolutely not!"

They both opened new windows on their respective computers and found a live feed from China on YouTube.

The screen showed the huge *Long March 10* rocket, with a countdown displayed accompanied by a Chinese voice-over. Elizabeth opened a translator bot so that she could hear it in English.

She then switched to the intercom and said, "Forget the space agencies. I want Lisa Lunn at the CIA, and I want to know why we weren't informed of this launch. I refuse to believe they didn't know about it."

Sir Atwater had muted the mic, and she suspected that he was making a similar call to MI6.

The YouTube channel went blank, and a message appeared to the effect that this channel was not available in her country.

Elizabeth took note of that, mentally commenting that her anticipated conversation with the CIA just got more interesting, and then launched a VPN, selected a server in Bangkok, and reopened YouTube only to find that the feed was still unavailable.

She opened her office door and looked out onto the common area. "Does anybody have a feed of the China launch?"

"Yes, Ma'am," a young woman said. "I've got China Central Television on the monitors." The young woman clicked her mouse a couple of times and the launch was again visible just as the countdown approached T-minus 10 seconds.

A voice counted from 10 to zero in Chinese and the huge rocket lifted off without incident.

"Ma'am," Elizabeth's secretary said. "The president is calling."

"I've got it," Elizabeth said and clicked her earpiece. The president's shrill, whiney voice made her stomach clench. She had decided years ago that she'd rather have sex with a cheese grater than listen to the president's voice.

"Liz, why didn't we know about this launch in China? We should have known about it. America needs to be the first one there."

"Why are you asking me? Ask the CIA or Space Force. We're not a spy agency."

"Liz, we have to be there first," the president repeated. "How long before we can launch?"

"That depends on how much we're being funded," Elizabeth lied, then said, " We can't get a rocket off the ground before August 20."

"That's not soon enough, Liz."

"Mr. President, we have nothing ready to launch, but we're working around the clock."

Traveler

"You're fired, Liz." The president hung up.

Morrison stood motionless for nearly a minute, wondering who was going to take her place. She knew with certainty that it would be somebody who'd get to the moon simply to curry the president's favor, and they wouldn't care who had to die to achieve that.

"Administrator?" her secretary said with concern in her voice.

"Not anymore, Rebecca. I just got my pink slip."

"But boss, how can he do that?"

Morrison shrugged and said, "He's the president."

• • •

WEDNESDAY, AUGUST 2
07:18 EDT
TIME SINCE TRAVELER ARRIVAL: 40 DAYS, 12 HOURS, 52 MINUTES
MORRISON RESIDENCE

Although it was old news by now that a rocket would head for the moon, the world held its collective breath as the *Lóngyuè-1*, the first crewed Chinese mission to the moon and the first spacecraft from Earth to attempt to rendezvous with the alien spaceship, approached Trans-Lunar Injection, that point in its orbit where it would ignite its engines and head for the moon.

And the world continued to hold its breath for several minutes after the ship failed to ignite its engines.

Elizabeth Morrison sat alone in her apartment in Logan Circle, with all the curtains closed and the remains of an attempted breakfast on the counter. She made do with coffee and toast. She had spent the morning like any other workday, rising at 4:00, showering, and getting dressed, but never leaving the apartment. She was an old hand when it came to launches, but she had never before felt so useless.

Three different television sets were tuned to different news stations, and the computer screen in her home office displayed the link from the Chinese news agency.

When the countdown for the TLI reached zero and nothing happened, news commentators worldwide resorted to speculation, but there was no word from Beijing.

Morrison turned one of the televisions to the local news, which was reporting on the flood damage from the high tide. Ronald Reagan Airport was closed, as well as the National Mall and the Lincoln Memorial. The news anchors were careful not to suggest that anthropogenic climate change had anything to do with higher tides, as per directives from the National Oceanic and Atmospheric Administration, under the direction of a presidential appointee and mega-donor.

Her cell phone buzzed. It was Bob Schoonover.

• • •

THURSDAY, AUGUST 3
13:42 EDT
TIME SINCE TRAVELER ARRIVAL: 41 DAYS, 19 HOURS, 17 MINUTES
NASA HQ, WASHINGTON, D.C.

After watching Radek Bostik and six scientists, personally picked by Bostik himself, launch into Earth Orbit on the rocket *MoonShot I*, Dr. Robert Schoonover called a meeting of the lead scientists, engineers, and astronauts. He had been named the interim NASA administrator as soon as Elizabeth Morrison had cleared out her office. Schoonover's first official act was to give Morrison a job as a consultant and invite her to the meeting.

The meeting room was large, with plush carpeting and a long faux-wood table running down the middle. Hot and cold water, hot coffee, and tea bags were available.

"Good afternoon," Dr. Schoonover addressed the group in his baritone voice while he pulled a pair of reading glasses from his suit jacket pocket. He quickly read some notes on a 3 x 5 card and then tore it up, letting the pieces fall on the floor. Morrison could tell that he was doing it for dramatic effect. He was standing at a lectern while everybody else was sitting at the table, signaling that he was in charge and would brook no nonsense. "I'm insisting that this meeting be unofficial," he continued. "No records, no recordings. You've all been required to leave your cell phones and laptops at the door. Any paper notes you make will be burned after the meeting, but we'll give you a few minutes to memorize them. Any questions? Good."

It did not go unnoticed that he gave less than two seconds for anybody to respond. He had other topics to discuss and he felt like time was speeding by at a break-neck pace.

Dr. Schoonover checked his watch. "Here's the deal: Since the traveler arrived, the administrators and chiefs of the world's major space agencies have all received text messages from an anonymous source with links to documents on an untraceable server, which give technical specifications on major technological breakthroughs. We've already discussed the information received by

Morrison and Sir Atwater regarding carbon sequestration and inexpensive high-capacity batteries. After lengthy discussions and negotiations, we've learned that the European Space Agency received documents on commercial fusion. Japan was given documents on the manufacture of exotic materials. The Italians received information on advanced portable water purification units. The German Aerospace Center has specifications for improving thin-film photovoltaic collectors — with as much as 80% efficiency." Somebody whistled in amazement. "The Indian Space Research Center was given a treasure trove of genetic research in the field of climate-resilient agriculture, including drought-resistant crops, precision farming, and sustainable practices.

"The Chinese and Russians refused to acknowledge that they had any secret anonymous communications, but our friends in various spy agencies think they now possess information on advanced healthcare and, possibly, longevity." Dr. Schoonover checked his watch again.

"And we believe that the traveler sent this information?" Larry Manix asked. Everyone turned to look at him, incredulous that he wasn't on the same page. "And why?"

"Thirteen eighty-two." Dr. Schoonover replied tersely, referring to the code text received by the chiefs of each space agency, which echoed a short-lived radio broadcast from the traveler. "Besides, nobody on Earth has this information. And it's all tied to technologies we need to survive climate change."

"Were all the documents in English or in local languages?" Manix asked.

Schoonover remained stoic, but Morrison placed the palm of her hand over her face.

"We know the German documents are in Hochdeutch," Schoonover explained. "The other agencies didn't elaborate on that. We assume they are in local languages."

"While this is all speculation," Morrison said, sitting up and placing her elbows on the table. She had a $50 silver pen in her hands that looked to be the victim of much abuse. "It would appear that the traveler has intimate and detailed knowledge of our technological status and native languages." She paused and looked around the table. Despite her employment status, everybody was looking at her. They all respected the woman who had been their boss just last week, and everyone could tell that she had something to say.

"I am convinced," she said emphatically. "That the traveler wants us to survive climate change. Additionally, it went to a lot of trouble to give information divided into the major high-tech countries. The traveler wants us to work together." By her expression, Morrison dared anybody to disagree with her.

"So, why don't all the countries come out and declare this publically?"

Morrison pointed to the portrait of The U.S. President on the wall. "Right-wing nationalists have taken control of so many countries. The German Chancelor is AfD. The French Prime Minister is *Rassemblement National*. After bowling over Ukraine, the Russian Federation is on the ascendency and has its eyes on Poland, Slovakia, and Hungary. The president is trying not only to take the U.S. out of NATO but to convince the rest of the European powers to abandon it. I don't need to continue, do I?"

Nobody responded, and everybody looked disheartened.

"Our counterparts across the globe took major security risks in sharing this information with us," Schoonover said, and checked his watch. "That's why this meeting is strictly off the books. Our lawyers tell us if we get caught sharing the information from the traveler, we'll all be looking at serious jail time. Though I want to point out that failure to disclose any information about the traveler is a violation of several international agreements."

"So, what are we going to do about this?" an engineer, Amanda Elston, asked.

"We are moving ahead with our current launch window of August 20," Schoonover said. "We are putting our most experienced astronauts through mission-specific training. The mission will be commanded by Commander Steven Silva." Schoonover waved a hand towards an athletically-built man in his 50s who waved at everybody. "We are assembling the rocket now in Florida. We are also in conversations with intelligence and diplomatic agencies regarding protocols for a First Contact."

"Any news on the *Lóngyuè-1?*" Silva asked, conveying a deep interest that almost everyone else in the room lacked.

"It's still in Earth orbit. Beijing hasn't released any official news. There are rumors of a rescue mission," Schoonover said.

"And *MoonShot I?*" Silva asked.

"Approaching TLI," Elston said while consulting her watch. "In fifteen minutes and twenty seconds."

"Let's watch it," Schoonover said.

Elston turned around, pointed a remote controller at the wall, and pressed a button. A 100-inch QLED TV screen descended from the ceiling and powered up. The screen divided itself up into eight different views from the Johnson Space Center in Texas, which was monitoring the *MoonShot*

I's flight, and another from the control room at *StarDrive* Mission Control in the Pacific. Another part of the screen showed an animation of the spacecraft in orbit. One section showed the interior of the craft and its seven inhabitants. Everybody was strapped in and awaiting the acceleration that would speed them toward the Moon. There was a lot of technical chatter as the pilot of *MoonShot I* went through checklists in preparation for engine ignition.

Conversations in the NASA conference room became whispers as people commented on what they saw.

At T-3 minutes, the pilot of the *MoonShot I* declared, "Mission Control, we have a failure on the ignition systems for engines 1, 5, and 7." After about five seconds, the pilot continued: "Mission Control, we have engine failure in all engines."

"*MoonShot I*, please hold," said CapCom. Then, "*MoonShot I*, we confirm failure in all engines."

"That's it," Elston said. "They can't achieve injection."

"Can they get back home?" Morrison asked.

There was more techno-chatter between *MoonShot I* and Mission Control as they tried to troubleshoot the problem. The abort protocol called for the crew capsule to fire the powerful abort rockets to deorbit, but those also failed.

"Maybe?" Elston answered Morrison, making it a question. "Like, they might be able to use the thrusters to slow enough to skip off the atmosphere a couple of times until they're going slow enough to deorbit, but, maybe they'd be better off trying to make it to the International Space Station. But, y'know," she made a vague gesture at the screen. "Something tells me that those will fail, too. If everything fails," Elston scrunched her eyebrows together and looked worried. "They have enough consumables to last a couple of weeks."

"What are the odds of every engine failing separately at the same time?" Morrison asked.

"That, like, depends on the problem," Elston said. "But overall, not very damn likely. Akin to pigs flying. They're designed to be redundant systems."

The window for TLI came and went, and after considerably more techno-chatter, CapCom announced that they would try again on the next orbit, in about 93 minutes.

The conversation at NASA turned quickly into spitballing ideas for a rescue.

Morrison had the kernel of an idea and became silent. Out of habit, she walked over to the coffee pot and poured herself a cup.

"Ms. Morrison, are you okay?" Elston asked, who had eased up to Morrison and tentatively touched her arm. "You've been standing here for, like, several minutes."

"The systems were all nominal until they announced their intention to accelerate towards the moon," Morrison said absently. "Then it all went sideways."

"Okay, and?"

"What if they announced that they wanted to deorbit and positioned their craft to do so?"

"I don't see how that would fix anything," Elston said, squishing her eyebrows together again. "The abort engines failed."

Morrison turned towards the meeting table and announced, "Somebody get me a link to *MoonShot I*. Call *StarDrive* Mission Control, tell them I want a radio link."

Instead of jumping up to fulfill Morrison's request

Traveler

as she expected them to, they just all sat there, looked at her, and then at Dr. Schoonover.

"You heard her," he said. "Get her a radio link!"

It was Elston who called the Space Center in Houston, who contacted *MoonShot I* via VHF radio. They eventually set up an audio/visual link, and everybody could see Bostik's contorted, angry face.

"Elizabeth. Have you called me to gloat?" Radek Bostik said in his odd accent. "I thought you got fired?"

"Radek, listen to me," she said, ignoring the comments. "You have to put your craft into re-entry mode, and announce that you are deorbiting."

"Elizabeth, what part of 'The engines are in-op' don't you understand? What do you hope to achieve?"

"Radek, do you want to spend a month in orbit with six other people in that crowded capsule, or do you want to come home?"

"Rhetorical question. There is no means of performing a deorbit burn."

"What have you got to lose?"

There was a long silence. Morrison imagined the conversation between Bostik, the pilot, and *Stellar Thrust's* Mission Control with Bostik getting pissed off, the pilot trying to accommodate his boss, and CapCom being the adult in the room. If it had been a NASA mission, this would have already been attempted.

"What are you thinking, Elizabeth?" Schoonover asked.

"What if the traveler doesn't want us to go to the moon, but it doesn't care if we return to Earth?"

"You think the traveler hacked the command systems of *Moonshot*?" Schoonover asked seriously. Morrison had always admired his ability to never sound surprised.

"Nobody had considered this, but the fact that the traveler had been able to infiltrate communications systems should have been a hint," Morrison explained. "And these incidents can't be a coincidence. First the Chinese — We know they have a robust rocket. Now *MoonShot I*. What are the odds? I'll bet a million bucks that the same thing will happen to our rocket, which is identical to *MoonShot*."

"Elizabeth," Bostek said after unmuting his mic. "I think you are bat-shit crazy, but Mission Control says we need to try."

After acknowledging, Dr. Schoonover muted the mic and told everybody in the room to go back to their desks and offices, and they would reconvene when *Moonshot I* was ready to deorbit.

As everybody stood up and prepared to leave the room, the door opened with a loud *thunk* of latches that startled everyone and only the hydraulic mechanism prevented it from slamming into the wall. A balding white man of medium height wearing eyeglasses, an expensive suit and an absurd but colorful tie strode in like a conquering warrior. To punctuate the sentiment, he was followed by four tough-looking Marines holding automatic weapons and a *Don't fuck with me* attitude.

"Everybody sit back down," the intruder said before anybody could object. "My name is Dr. Lloyd Markus, and I'm now in charge of this chicken shit operation."

"Dr. Markus," Dr. Schoonover eyed the Marines and their weapons and said, "You'd better have some serious paperwork with you because this is as irregular as it gets."

Markus walked to the lectern and brushed aside the paperwork that was there. Papers fluttered to the ground and a notebook flew across the room.

"My first order of business," he said, looking at a sheet of paper, "is to fire, again, Elizabeth Morrison. Just whose idea was it to bring her back in after the president specifically threw her out of the agency?"

There was silence as everybody except for Marcus looked at Dr. Schoonover.

"Well?" Markus said and looked up. "Speak up, or be charged with impeding a government operation."

"Paperwork, Dr. Markus. Or it didn't happen," Schoonover said with a determined, measured voice.

"Fine." Markus turned to the marines and pointed to Schoonover. "Remove this person and put him in holding. Which one of you is Morrison?"

"You've got to be kidding!" Schoonover protested as he was being forced-marched from the room. "How can you have lived outside of a cave in the Amazon and not recognize her by sight? She's been on the news daily for over a month!"

After the door closed behind Schoonover, Markus pointed at Amanda Elston seemingly at random and said, "Speak up."

Elston responded by shrugging her shoulders and making a vague gesture.

"Remove this person, too," Markus said to the Marines, and they moved to pick her up.

Defiant, Amanda stood up and started marching herself out of the room. "I know when my talents are better appreciated somewhere else." She pointed at one of the Marines and said, "Touch me and die!"

This did not deter the corporal from grabbing her arm and forcing her towards the door. As the door closed behind her, she could be heard promising to sue the entire military for violating her civil rights.

"Make sure she signs the Non-Compete Agreement," Markus said, just to be mean.

"She's Morrison," Larry Manix said and pointed without waiting to be addressed.

"Finally, somebody sees sense!" Markus nearly shouted. "Elizabeth Morrison, I'm placing you under arrest on suspicion of espionage, specifically 18 U.S.C. Section 794(a) and (b). Read her her rights and take her into custody."

• • •

SATURDAY, AUGUST 5, PROBABLY.
TIME UNKNOWN
TIME SINCE TRAVELER ARRIVAL: MAYBE 43 DAYS
CENTRAL DETENTION FACILITY, WASHINGTON, D.C.

Elizabeth Morrison sat alone in a single cell at the Central Detention Facility in Washington, D.C. The Marines had dropped her off without ceremony, and she'd been booked, strip-searched, given prison garb, fingerprinted, and photographed. Other than giving them her name, the only thing Elizabeth told them was that she wanted to see a lawyer, but the guards made it clear that they didn't care.

The guards brought food, which she ate sitting on the cot, but they otherwise ignored her. Nobody questioned her. They had taken all her belongings, including her watch, so she had no idea what time it was or how long she'd been there. The guards had brought her six meals, so she assumed it was Saturday afternoon, and further assumed that she'd be arraigned on Monday. However, those were only assumptions, which were worth very little in an era of extrajudicial political retaliations. The president, after forcing the Senate and the House to impeach all the justices who might obstruct his plans, had the Supreme Court in his pocket. The majority of state legislatures took their marching orders from that executive. She had no doubt that she was in jail at the whim of the president.

She knew that the Central Detention Facility had been the subject of considerable criticism. There was that 2017 report by the Human Rights Commission that described it as a "place of human suffering." Overcrowding and understaffing were at the top of the list of complaints, and things had only gotten worse since. So, the fact that she was in a cell by herself spoke volumes to Elizabeth. They didn't want her to interact with other prisoners.

The room had four solid concrete walls and a hefty steel door with a small window through which the meals arrived. The room itself was perhaps eight feet by ten feet and contained a metal bed, a toilet, and a sink. A security camera that covered the entire space. There was also a vent through which she could hear things that made it sound like something was falling apart. She half expected the air conditioning to quit at any moment.

The first thing she did after the cell door closed was to find the security camera. She looked directly at it and repeated her demand to talk to her lawyer. When the first meal was delivered, she asked the guard when she would be allowed to make a phone call, but they just ignored her. Then she spent the next several hours wondering just what the hell was going on, but she had a good idea: She had told the president "No" and now she was paying for it. She didn't have any reading material, so she sat on the cot, lay on the cot, walked around the cramped cell, and worried about her colleagues at the office, but boredom set in eventually. She tried to sleep as much as possible.

She occupied herself by playing all the piano music she could remember in her mind. She sat on the cot, put her hands on an air piano, and did her best to remember each arpeggio and melody. Then she stood up, paced the cell, and remembered all the great hikes she'd been on. She imagined the trails as she walked them in her mind.

She started calculating the distance. She estimated the cell was ten feet long, which meant that there were 264 laps to the mile.

She quickly lost count of the laps, but she estimated that she walked twenty-five miles when a lawyer — not hers — entered.

"Good afternoon, Ms. Morrison. I'm Bill Beckman. I've been sent here on the behest of the president to represent you."

"I want my own lawyer," she said.

"And I'm truly sorry to report that your counsel has also been detained on conspiracy charges. He's already confessed to aiding and abetting you."

"Bullshit. And why should I trust a lawyer supplied by the president?"

Beckman laughed mirthlessly. "In truth, you shouldn't. But I'm the only advocate you're getting."

"I have the right to hire my own lawyer!"

"Not anymore you don't."

Elizabeth had no idea what to say to that, but finally managed, "I'm going to sue you, the person who hired

Traveler

you, and every guard on this block into insolvency if I don't get some satisfaction."

"Please sit down, Ms. Morrison, and I will endeavor to explain to you the facts of life." Beckman's face was serious. "It's not like you have much of a choice."

Feeling confrontational, Elizabeth leaned against the wall, making it obvious that she had no intention of sitting.

"Fine," Beckman said and shrugged. "It doesn't change anything. Let's get started." He pulled a file out of his attaché case and laid it on the cot.

"Why are we having this conversation in a cell?" Elizabeth asked. "I suspect this video will be all over YouTube by dinner," she said, pointing at the camera. "I have a right to privacy when talking to a lawyer."

Beckman ignored her. "On Monday morning, you'll be arraigned at the U.S. District Court here. You'll be charged under 18 U.S.C. Section 794. Specifically, for gathering or delivering defense information to aid a foreign government. This is a serious crime that is punishable by death or by imprisonment for any term of years or for life.

"You have two choices," Beckman said gravely. "You can plead not guilty and face criminal liability of as much as the DA wants to throw at you, or you can plead guilty, and you'll serve two years at a minimum security facility, and ten years probation."

Elizabeth wasn't stupid. The unspoken part of Beckman's message was that she was going to be found guilty regardless.

"I remember when there was a presumption of innocence," she said.

Beckman frowned, sighed, and said quietly, "We all do." He pulled out a pen and gave it to Elizabeth. "Do you need me to say it? Alright, the president has declared martial law and rescinded *habeas corpus*. Sucks to be you."

Elizabeth silently considered her options, and Beckman was patient enough to give her a few minutes. "What time is it now?"

Beckman looked at his watch, then said happily, "Ten-thirty in the morning on a mostly sunny Sunday."

"Do you expect me to sign these documents now?" Elizabeth asked gloomily.

"I'll leave them here, but I can't leave you a pen. You've been placed on suicide watch," he said as he took the pen back.

Elizabeth had tried to keep her cool, but her anger at the situation rose as bile in her throat. She clenched her fists and tightened her jaw. Her only goal in that moment was to kick Beckman between the legs and then stuff the documents into all of his orifices. But adding murder charges to the list would only make her captors happier. Instead, she closed her eyes and counted to 10. Then again in Spanish, and again in German, and again in Latin. She was about to start counting in Korean when Beckman broke the spell.

"I'll be back after dinner, or tomorrow at the latest."

"One more thing," Elizabeth said, stopping him with a hand on his sleeve. "What happened to the *Moonshot* crew?"

Beckman just smiled and said, "Have a good evening, Ms. Morrison."

He called for the guard and was let out almost instantly.

• • •

SATURDAY, AUGUST 5
TIME: SEVERAL HOURS AFTER BECKMAN'S VISIT
TIME SINCE TRAVELER ARRIVAL: 43 DAYS

After being too angry and worried to eat lunch, Elizabeth sat on the cot with her back to the wall and somehow fell asleep. She woke up to buzzing and clicking sounds and a terrible crick in the neck. She opened her eyes and swatted the air, thinking that mosquitos or large flies had come into the cell. She looked around for bugs, and at first, didn't see any.

Then she noticed the security camera, or at least where it should have been. All that remained was the end of a coax cable hanging from the ceiling. Then she heard more clicking and buzzing as a strange-looking insect flew in through the air vent. It was about half an inch long and had wings longer than the body. It flew to the ground and made the clicking sound.

Elizabeth pulled her legs up next to her butt and cautiously looked over the edge of the cot. There, in the middle of the floor was something black and rectangular containing circuitry. It was about the size of a cell phone.

As she watched, two more insects flew in, rendezvoused with the rectangular thing, and joined it. They simply joined with the object, flexed, and seamlessly became part of the object with a click as if the insect never existed.

Fascinated, she edged closer for a better look. More insects came in, and she could see that they were mechanical things. Not bugs at all. More flew through the air vent and merged with the box.

After about twenty minutes, the mechanical bugs had formed what was, without any doubt, a cell phone. Once the buzzing and clicking were done, it lay on the floor like some puzzle calling her name. As she reached out tentatively to touch it, she felt like one of the hominins who dared to touch the monolith in that movie from the sixties.

Okay, now what? Elizabeth wondered.

It booted up. A logo showing a stylized spaceship orbiting a stylized moon was displayed for about ten seconds, and then the screen went dark again. When the screen reappeared, it displayed a telephone interface.

It didn't surprise her in the least when it rang, but she nearly jumped off the bed. She was reluctant to pick it up, worried that it would transform into a swarm of flying mechanical bugs. It rang again, and Elizabeth reached her hands toward it and brushed her fingers along the side. It felt cool and metallic. It kept ringing, and Elizabeth was worried that the noise would attract the guards. The display showed that the caller was 1382. The traveler. Who else could have done this?

Elizabeth stood up and then reached down to pick up the phone. She pressed Accept and the image of an average-looking caucasian woman, probably 30 years old, appeared on the screen.

"Hello, Elizabeth."

"Uh, hello," Elizabeth managed to sputter. "I guess?" The image of the woman was the last thing she thought the traveler would look like. "You look very human."

There was about a three-second lag before the woman said, "Oh, yeah, this is just a virtual image. A filter, if you will. This way, I can appear and sound like different people on Earth, depending on whom I'm speaking with. When I contact China, for instance, I will look completely different."

"That …" Elizabeth was on the verge of freaking out, and she struggled to say something that sounded intelligent. "… makes sense, actually. But why are you calling me? You went to a lot of trouble to do it."

There was another three-second lag, and Elizabeth realized that this was the light travel delay between the Earth and the Moon. "I felt like you deserved an explanation. You've lost your job and now you're going to prison just for trying to make your leaders behave in a sensible way to my visit. I also wanted to give you an update on the *Moonshot I* mission. You'll be happy to know that your idea worked and that both they and the Chinese are safely on the ground."

Elizabeth let out a breath that she felt she had been holding all weekend. "Thank you. But that doesn't seem like it was worth building a cell phone on the floor."

The woman smirked and turned away for a few seconds. She turned back to the screen and said, "I also wanted to let you know that we are taking your planet. It's valuable real estate, and we want it."

"You're invading," Elizabeth choked and swallowed. This was the president's worst fear, and she had enabled it.

"No," the woman said. "There's no need to. We can see how things are going both politically and environmentally on Earth. Our experts give you between 50 and 100 years, and the entire planet will be uninhabitable for Terran life. Climate change is a bitch, right? After you're gone, we'll send in the machines to remake the Earth to our liking. Your species won't be alive to object."

Elizabeth was speechless. She closed her eyes and thought about the climate-driven armageddon that was happening. She finally said, "We'll all be dead, and you won't have to pull a single trigger. We are committing suicide by climate change."

"Not only that," the woman said. "But opportunistic diseases and wars driven by shrinking resources will likely be the final nails in your existential coffin."

Elizabeth sat down heavily on the cot. "How can you just sit there in orbit and watch us die? Why can't you help us? You have terraforming machines, you could help us repair the environment."

"I did try to help," the woman said. "I gave you opportunities."

"Oh, yes," Elizabeth remembered now. All of the technical documents that had been sent to various space agencies. "Why did you send those documents if you want us to die?"

"Who said we want you to die? But if you're going to put a gun to your own head, we can't stop you. And how your governments handled those documents cemented the deal. Your president has classified all communications between us, and you're in prison for trying to share them. Your government is controlled by a religion that believes the End Times have arrived, and that it's God's plan. As long as your government is controlled by what your own pundits call a doomsday cult, the result is inevitable."

Elizabeth was silent again, and after about thirty seconds, the woman broke the silence with, "Is there anything I can do for you?"

"You can get me out of this prison."

"Are you sure you want to spend the rest of your life on the lam?"

"Are you kidding? I have no intention of watching this slow-motion apocalypse from inside a jail cell. If we only have fifty years left, I can think of a lot of better places to spend them."

"But the DA has offered you a deal. Sign the letters, do your two-year incarceration, and then get out."

"Do you really think the DA will honor this? And even if he does, There's nothing to prevent the judge from throwing out the agreement. I'm not stupid. I've made a lot of political enemies."

"No," the woman said. "You're not stupid. So, I'll tell you what. I can't break you out of jail, but I can send an opportunity your way. Recognize it, and take it, and you'll be out before breakfast."

"WAIT! What opportunity?"

"Goodbye, Elizabeth. I wish you the best."

The cell phone went dark.

It occurred to Elizabeth that she could use the cell phone to call Bob Schoonover, but the phone dissolved into a thousand flying mechanical things that flew through the air vent.

• • •

SATURDAY, AUGUST 5
TIME: IMMEDIATELY AFTER THE JAILHOUSE CONVERSATION
TIME SINCE TRAVELER ARRIVAL: 43 DAYS

In a spacecraft orbiting the Moon, a solitary brown-haired human woman of indeterminate ethnicity sat at a communications console. The voice of the ship's artificial intelligence came over the room's speakers. "You really pressed the boundaries of the rules there. Stretched them to nearly the breaking point."

"Yes, but I didn't break them, and I expect your report to reflect that fact," the woman said softly. She had started this mission without much hope of success, and the events that followed didn't elevate her expectations.

"I predict a near certainty," the AI said, "that this Earth will follow the same path as our own planet: biosphere collapse in fifty to a hundred years. The last decades of this civilization will be spent fighting over clean water, food, and oxygen. Then our employers can take over."

"A famous man once said, 'It ain't over 'till it's over.'"

"I'm unfamiliar with that quote."

"It was said by a baseball legend, Yogi Berra. His team was way behind in the standings, but they eventually rallied to win the division title."

"And you're hoping that this Earth can pull off a Yogi Berra?" The AI seemed amused at the thought.

"I gave them opportunities."

"You gave them shortcuts," the AI insisted with a tinge of anger. "I should have put a stop to the program then."

"No. I did not give them any new technologies. I simply showed them how to use existing technologies in new ways. That is entirely allowed by the rules."

"Barely," the AI scoffed. "And what *'opportunity'* are you going to give Administrator Morrison?"

"A sleepy guard, a power failure, and a little help from her friends."

"What friends?"

The woman smiled and said, "Let me show you something I found." She reached for a computer keyboard. This command had to be given silently. She entered a simple three-line command that called and executed an emergency override procedure.

Traveler

When the *Task Completed* icon appeared on the screen, she said, "Give me a countdown from ten."

There was nothing. She heard the air coming from the overhead vent, and she heard the gentle rumble of the power generators, but no computer voice. Of course, once the ship's AI failed to report on schedule to her employers, she'd be screwed. But that would take years.

"Time for a ride to the surface. Yogi Berra, here I come."

ABOUT THE AUTHOR

Andrea Monticue lives with her wife and their dog in rural Oregon, where she designs spaceships, imagines alien worlds, practices her sword and archery skills, and studies languages, anthropology, math, and music. She's not very good at any of it, but keeps practicing anyway. She has retired from her life as an interstellar spy and occasionally writes about her adventures and submits them to clueless publishers.

YOU MIGHT ALSO ENJOY

O2
Kellyn Solvera

Restored to life in a future world where access to the very air he breathes is rationed, a man attempts to break free from the governmental restraints, only to discover why the government now regulates everything.

FLAWLESS
J. Scott Coatsworth

When someone tries to steal one of Greyson's mining scores, he has half a mind to just toss the guy off his rock and into open space. But that all changes when he discovers the stranger's identity ... and that he knows Greyson's secret.

LITTLE GREEN MEN
Curtis Bass

In an orbiting craft, Cooper has a front row seat to the first manned mission to Mars. Their landing is perfect until one crew member claims they are being watched by indigenous creatures.

Available in digital and trade paperback editions from
Water Dragon Publishing
waterdragonpublishing.com

Milton Keynes UK
Ingram Content Group UK Ltd.
UKHW040638131024
449481UK00001B/24